ALL BY MYSELF

BY MERCER MAYER

A GOLDEN BOOK • NEW YORK

Western Publishing Company, Inc., Racine, Wisconsin 53404

I can get out of bed
all by myself.

I can button
my overalls.

I can brush my fur.

I can put on my socks…

and tie my shoes.

I can pour some juice
for my little sister...

and help her eat breakfast.

I can pull a duck for her.

I can drive my truck.

I can ride my bike.

I can give a drink
to my bear.

I can kick my ball…

and roll on the ground.

I can pound with my hammer.

I can sail my boat.

I can look after
my little sister.

I can help Dad
trim a bush…

or ice a cake for Mom.

I can look at a
book and find
a mouse.

I can color a picture.

I can put my toys away…

and get into my pajamas.

I can brush my teeth.

I can put myself to bed...

but I can't go to sleep
without a story.

Good night.